'TWAS THE
NIGHT BEFORE
CHRISTMAS

Dedicated to Santa's Little
Helpers everywhere.
—JC

'TWAS THE NIGHT BEFORE CHRISTMAS

ADAPTED FROM THE POEM BY
CLEMENT C. MOORE

PICTURES BY
JANE CHAPMAN

sourcebooks
jabberwocky

'TWAS THE NIGHT BEFORE CHRISTMAS,

When all through the house
Not a creature was stirring, not even a mouse;

The stockings were hung by the chimney with care,
In hopes that St. Nicholas soon would be there;

The children were nestled all snug in their beds;
While visions of sugar-plums danced in their heads;
And Mama in her kerchief, and I in my cap,
Had just settled our heads for a long winter's nap,

When out on the lawn there arose such a clatter,
I sprang from my bed to see what was the matter.
Away to the window I flew like a flash,
Tore open the shutters and threw up the sash.

The moon on the breast of the new-fallen snow,
Gave a luster of midday to objects below,
When what to my wondering eyes did appear,
But a miniature sleigh and eight tiny dog-deer,

With a polar bear driver so lively and quick,
I knew in a moment he must be St. Nick.

More rapid than eagles his canines they came,
And he whistled, and shouted, and called them by name:

"NOW, DASHER! NOW, DANCER! NOW PRANCER AND VIXEN! ON, COMET! ON, CUPID! ON DONNER AND BLITZEN!

To the top of the porch! To the top of the wall!
Now dash away, dash away, dash away all!"

As dry leaves that before the wild hurricane fly,
When they meet with an obstacle, mount to the sky;
So up to the housetop the puppies they flew
With the sleigh full of toys, and St. Nicholas too—
And then, in a twinkling, I heard on the snow

The prancing and pawing of each little toe.
As I drew in my head, and was turning around,
Down the chimney St. Nicholas came with a bound.
He was dressed all in fur, from his head to his foot,
And his clothes were all tarnished with ashes and soot;
A bundle of toys he had flung on his back,
And he looked like a peddler just opening his pack.

His eyes—how they twinkled! His dimples, how merry!
His cheeks were like roses, his nose like a cherry!
His droll little mouth was drawn up like a bow,
And the beard on his chin was as white as the snow;

He had a broad face and a giant round belly
That shook when he laughed, like a bowl full of jelly.
He was chubby and plump, a right jolly old elf,
And I laughed when I saw him, in spite of myself;

A wink of his eye and a twist of his head
Soon gave me to know I had nothing to dread;
He spoke not a word, but went straight to his work,
And filled all the stockings; then turned with a jerk,

And laying his paw to one side of his nose,
And giving a nod, up the chimney he rose;

He sprang to his sleigh, to his team gave a whistle,
And away they all flew like the down of a thistle.
But I heard him exclaim, ere he drove out of sight—

"MERRY CHRISTMAS TO ALL, AND TO ALL A GOOD NIGHT!"

THE ORIGINS OF
'TWAS THE NIGHT BEFORE CHRISTMAS

'Twas the Night Before Christmas, originally known as *A Visit from St. Nicholas*, is perhaps the best known verse ever written by an American author. It is a timeless work of poetry which has heralded the excitement and joy of Christmastime for generations.

'Twas the Night Before Christmas was first published on December 23, 1823, in *The Troy Sentinel*, a regional New York newspaper. The poem is widely attributed with helping to establish the modern traits of Santa Claus; having a jolly personality, a round belly and a beard as "white as snow."

Although first published anonymously, the poem was later attributed to Clement Clarke Moore, an American writer and professor from New York City. Moore is thought to have originally written the poem to entertain his six children.

Copyright © 2022, 2024 by Sourcebooks

Adapted from the poem by Clement C. Moore
Text revisions by Josalyn Moran, Jane Chapman, and Andrew Hogan
Illustrations by Jane Chapman
Book designed by Nick Tiemersma
Cover and internal design © 2024 by Sourcebooks

Sourcebooks and the colophon are registered trademarks of Sourcebooks.

The full colour art was created using acrylic paints on paper.

Published by Sourcebooks Jabberwocky, an imprint of Sourcebooks Kids
P.O. Box 4410, Naperville, Illinois 60567-4410
(630) 961-3900
sourcebookskids.com

Originally published as 'Twas the Night Before Christmas in 2022 in the United States of America by Dan Dee International, LLC.

Cataloging-in-Publication Data is on file with the Library of Congress.

Source of Production: Wing King Tong Paper Products Co. Ltd., Shenzhen, Guangdong Province, China
Date of Production: April 2024
Run Number: 5039094

Printed and bound in China.
WKT 10 9 8 7 6 5 4 3 2 1